WELCOME TO GREYSTONE

WELCOME TO GREYSTONE

M.P. GLENN

CONTENTS

To my parents Patricia and Milton—
You planted this dream and taught me to grow it.

Mommy—You turned my "what ifs" into "why nots." You treated every idea like it mattered and every page like it could be something. Your encouragement didn't just help me write this book—it set the tone for the stories still to come. Whenever I reach for courage, I hear your voice first. This book carries your love and belief on every line, and in many books to come.

Daddy—You've been there—steady, present, and proud—cheering in the loud moments and standing close in the quiet ones. You taught me to keep going, to keep striving and pushing foreward and to celebrate each step. With all my love, I place this first book in your hands as a gift for your 65th birthday. May it show you what your love and faith in me has built.
Happy Birthday Daddy!

Together, you gave me both roots and wings.
This book is the proof—and the beginning.

- With All My Love, Your Daughter

CHAPTER I

Newcomers

The last morning in Virginia was bright and restless. Boxes crowded every corner of the Lynn household, taped shut and labeled in Maria's neat handwriting. The air smelled faintly of coffee and packing tap "Do we really have to leave?" Mila asked, clutching her plush snow cone cat as movers carried out the last of the furniture. Her big eyes darted nervously from the empty living room to the open front door, as though something might slip away and stay behind forever.

"You'll make new friends, sweet pea," Maria said, kneeling to gently pull the loose braids from her youngest daughter's cheek back into a pony tail. Her voice was gentle but filled with certainty. "And you'll still have the same snow cone cat to keep you company." Maliyah, leaning against the banister, crossed her arms. "I already had friends here," she muttered. "What if people in Greystone are... weird?"

Roland, lugging a box marked "KITCHEN" out to the moving truck, chuckled. "Sweetheart, people are weird every-where. At least in a small town, they're easier to figure out." Maria shot him a look, though she smiled. "Not helping."

Still, both parents were buzzing with excitement, though it was different from their daughters'. For Maria, a fresh assignment at the local hospital promised a new chapter in her career as a psychiatrist.

For Roland, it was the chance to finally build something of his own—a law firm with his name on the door. The move wasn't just about leaving Virginia. It was about starting again. Hours later, the family car wound its way through the mist-drenched cliffs that welcomed them to Greystone. Maria pressed her palm to the car window as if to memorize the view. "It's smaller than Richmond," she said, smiling. "I think I can get used to a small town."

"Yeah," Roland agreed. "A small town means less complicated clients and drama." Maliyah leaned forward from the back seat, watching the town unfold outside her window. Narrow streets curled into one another, and shadows clung to the edges of old brick buildings. Streetlamps flickered even though the sun was still up. Mila frowned and drew a small heart on the foggy glass.

"Why does everything look... creepy?" Mila asked softly. Maliyah nodded in agreement. "It feels like the kind of place where people tell ghost stories and actually mean them." Before either could dwell on the thought, Maria's voice cut through, warm and steady.

"Look at those little shops," she said, pointing out a bakery with a striped awning and a general store with jars of candy in the window. "And the woods—aren't they beautiful? And the ocean's right there. We'll have picnics by the shore." Still, the girls exchanged uneasy glances. It was hard to ignore how

the fog seemed to linger like it had nowhere else to be. As the car curved up a winding road, the silhouette of a massive stone building came into view. Blackwood Hollow Academy.

Both girls fell silent, staring wide-eyed at its gothic spires and ivy-wrapped walls. The windows stretched tall and narrow, like unblinking eyes, and the tower rose higher than the trees around it. The bell, dark as thunderclouds, hung in its arch. Even from a distance, the school looked haunted—like a place built for secrets, not children.

"That's it," Maria said proudly. "Your new school. Elementary on one side, middle school on the other." But Maliyah and Mila didn't answer. They just kept staring until the car turned the corner and the building disappeared behind the trees. Their new home sat perched on a hill just outside town, isolated, with the vast ocean stretching endlessly in the background. The Victorian's cream paint and moss-green trim looked softened by the mist. Roses sprawled across the porch railing, and a wooden swing rocked lightly as if someone had just stepped off.

"Home," Roland said, his voice laced with both relief and anticipation. He climbed the steps, the key turning smoothly in the lock, and pushed the door open to reveal shiny wood floors and freshly painted walls. Inside, the air was cool and still. Maliyah, breaking the fresh paint from the windowsill, opened the bay window wide and breathed the outside in.

The air smelled of sea salt and fresh-cut grass, mingled together in a pleasant exhale. She held the breath a little longer than usual, as though memorizing the mix. Upstairs, Mila dropped her backpack in the room with the triangular closet. She sat cross-legged on the floor, hugging her plush cat tight. "It's a fairy house!" she screamed so everyone could hear her down the hallway. Maliyah laughed from her room.

"Only you would think a creepy closet is for fairies." "Fairies or not, it's mine," Mila shot back, grinning. Later that evening, they ate pizza on paper plates at the kitchen island, laughter and conversation bouncing between bites of melted cheese. On the back of a delivery receipt, they made a to-do list in Roland's bold handwriting:

- Grocery Store
- Library card
- Hardware store
- Rug for Mila's fairy closet

And in thick, underlined letters:
<u>Blackwood Hollow Academy – Enrollment Packets</u>

The next morning smelled of coffee and ocean air. Roland straightened his tie three times before they left the house. "You look fine," Maria said, slipping her arm through his. "More than fine. You look like a man ready to build something new." Roland grinned but glanced at the small poster board sign tucked in his briefcase:

ROLAND LYNN, ATTORNEY AT LAW. It wasn't much yet, but it was a beginning. The girls sat in the backseat, Mila swinging her legs and Maliyah leaning her chin against the window.

The road dipped towards Greystone Town Square, where the buildings pressed close together like they'd been standing shoulder-to-shoulder for ages. Maria pulled up in front of a brick building with tall windows. "Here it is," she said. "Your very own law firm." "Not bad, huh?" Roland rubbed his palms against his slacks before stepping out. "You girls behave. Don't let your mom buy out the bakery without me." They laughed as he disappeared inside, shaking hands with a landlord in suspenders.

Maria turned the car toward the square. "Let's see what this town has to offer." At first glance, Greystone was picturesque. The flower shop spilled color onto the sidewalk, and a cafe's chalkboard promised the best blueberry muffins in the county. People waved as they passed—an old man tipping his hat, a woman in an apron offering them a sample cookie. But through the girls' eyes, the shine dulled. Near the edge of the square, a man in a black coat stood perfectly still, staring at a wall where no sign hung. When Mila blinked, he was gone.

Two children played hopscotch by the fountain, but their chant was odd—numbers falling out of order, skipping ahead like they were reciting a rhyme only they understood. And in the bakery window, Maliyah thought she saw a face behind the glass, pale and frowning. Frightened, she looked away quickly, and when she turned back, the shutters were closed. "Everyone seems nice, right?" Maria asked, balancing a paper bag of muffins. "Much friendlier than Richmond." Mila clutched her plush cat tighter.

"If you say so..." Blackwood Hollow Academy loomed larger in daylight. Up close, the ivy seemed darker, its tendrils

curling like claws against the stone. The arch above the door bore carved leaves, their edges sharp and curling. Maria walked briskly to the front steps, smiling at a woman who stepped forward with a jangling key ring. "You must be the Lynns," the woman said.

Her smile was bright, her lipstick perfectly even. "I'm Ms. Alvarez. Welcome to Blackwood." Her tone was warm, but her eyes lingered too long on the girls, as if measuring something that couldn't be written on paper. Maliyah shifted under the gaze, and Mila stepped closer to her sister. Inside, the lobby smelled faintly of something older, like rainwater left in stone.

A goldfish swam in a round bowl on the counter, circling and circling. "Here are your enrollment packets," Ms. Alvarez said, sliding folders across the desk. "Schedules, supply lists, maps. Orientation is on Thursday." Her smile never faltered, but the air felt thin, like the hush before a storm. On their way out, Maliyah dropped her folder, and a boy stooped quickly to pick it up.

His hands were ink-stained, a spiral notebook clutched to his side. "Here," he said. His name—Andrew—was scribbled across the cover. He smiled briefly, but his eyes kept flicking to the high windows. Later, in the courtyard, they passed a boy sitting on the fountain's edge, skateboard leaning against his knee. He tilted his head toward the bell tower. "You hear it too sometimes, don't you?" His voice was casual, but his eyes were sharp. "I'm Zech." The girls waved and continued on, glancing at each other as if they had questions they knew they couldn't ask aloud.

In the library wing, two girls sat tucked between shelves: Tamia, her light brown hair parted slightly to the left and tucked neatly behind her ears, round black-framed glasses slipping down her nose as she sketched a pattern in her notebook; and Faith, humming while tracing her finger along an old hymnal. Both glanced up as the Lynns passed, their eyes catching just long enough to feel like recognition.

In the elementary hall, Mila nearly bumped into a boy balancing three toy dinosaurs. "Careful," he laughed. "They bite." His name was Branden, and his laugh was infectious. Beside him, a quiet girl named Journey sketched the school's tower with swift strokes.

She looked up just briefly, her eyes soft and kind, yet quietly observant. Leaving the academy, the girls felt a creeping unease as though someone, or something, was watching their exit in anticipation of their return. Back in the car, Mila whispered, "I think I'd rather be home schooled," clutching her plush cat tighter than before. Maliyah didn't answer right away.

She kept her eyes on the tower in the rearview mirror until it disappeared behind the mist. "We could wish all we want," she murmured, "but I doubt it'll do us any good." The Lynns believed they were stepping into a new life, but Greystone had been waiting—watching. The mist curled tighter around Blackwood Hollow as if sealing a secret, and the Academy towered above them like a beast waiting to strike.

CHAPTER II

The Blurred Face Child

Sound of water broke the air before the girls even stepped inside—a splash, a whistle, laughter bouncing against tile and glass. Maliyah and Mila entered the gymnasium pool together, towels clutched tight, the smell of chlorine sharp in their noses. Sunlight poured through the high windows, scattering diamonds across the water. "Wow..." Mila gasped, her eyes wide, "It's huge."

Their mother guided them forward, her hand on their backs. "Just relax. It's only tryouts," Maria said with a smile before heading toward the bleachers. The coach, tall and broad-shouldered with a whistle slung around his neck, paced along the edge of the pool. His voice carried easily.

"Alright, junior swimmers to the far lanes. Elementary to the shallow end." Maliyah shifted nervously, clutching her towel. The juniors gathered at the diving blocks, and among them she spotted Zech, the boy she and Mila had met by the fountain. He gave her a quick grin. "Guess we're teammates now."

Mila, meanwhile, drifted toward the shallow lanes, hugging her snow-cone plush cat until she spotted Branden stacking his dinosaur toys on the bleachers. Journey sat nearby, sketchbook balanced on her knees, glancing up between strokes of her pencil. The whistle shrilled. The pool erupted in motion—water foaming with kicks, splashes ricocheting off the walls.

Maliyah's stomach tightened as she stepped up onto the block. Her reflection trembled in the shifting blue below. "Next!" the coach barked. She bent her knees, filled her lungs, and dove. Cold wrapped around her body, shocking her skin. She kicked hard, arms slicing forward, the lane rope gliding past in blurred streaks. For a moment she felt strong, steady—until something else rippled in the depths underneath her. A shadow.

A pale outline. A boy's face, blurred by the water, staring up from below. Her chest tightened. She blinked hard, stroking faster, but the image clung to her mind. By the time she surfaced, gasping for air, her heart was hammering louder than the coach's whistle. "Good form," he said, jotting notes without looking up. "Next." Maliyah pushed her wet hair back, scanning the water. She told herself it was only a trick of the light. Only reflections. But across the pool, Mila was watching with wide eyes, holding her plush cat tighter. Because she had seen it too.

Mila dipped her toes into the shallow end, shivering as the water touched her skin. The elementary swimmers splashed around her, chattering nervously, but she stood still for a moment, staring at her reflection. The plush cat sat safely on the bleachers beside Branden's dinosaurs, as if they were keeping guard for her. "Ready?" the assistant coach asked, crouching down with a clipboard. Mila nodded, though her heart fluttered. She wasn't scared of swimming—just the water itself, the way it seemed to stretch wider and darker when she looked too long.

She slid in carefully, the pool wrapping her in cool silence. "Front crawl, two lengths," the assistant coach instructed. Mila pushed off. Her arms moved the way Maria had taught her in the community pool back in Richmond, her legs kicking small splashes. She was doing well, until halfway across the lane when the water beneath her rippled unnaturally. The tiles blurred, twisting into shapes. For an instant, she thought she saw fingers dragging across the pool floor, reaching upward, distorting her reflection. Her throat closed.

She jerked her head up, gasping, and paddled frantically to the edge. The assistant coach frowned. "You alright, kiddo?" Mila forced a nod, gripping the wall with both hands. Her heart hammered like it might escape her chest. She didn't dare look down again.

On the bleachers, Journey had stopped sketching. She was staring at Mila, her pencil hovering in the air. Branden's dinosaurs tumbled to the floor as he leaned forward, wide-eyed. And when Mila finally pulled herself out of the water, she didn't glance back at the pool once. Across the lanes, sitting on the bleachers, Maliyah's eyes met with her sister's. Neither said a word. They didn't have to. They had both seen something.

The splash echoed in the gymnasium as the last student climbed out of the pool. "You both did great," Maria said from the bleachers, clapping her hands together. Roland gave them a proud nod, though his tie was crooked from tugging at it all morning. "Best effort is all that matters," he said. "And you both gave it." The girls beamed. Even if their strokes weren't perfect, they'd tried, and the coaches had welcomed them onto the junior and elementary swim teams. Maria and Roland hugged them quickly before gathering their things. "We'll see you at home," Maria promised. "Don't forget to eat lunch."

The girls watched their parents leave, then followed the stream of students heading toward the cafeteria. The cafeteria was loud and warm, the air thick with the smell of mashed potatoes and gravy. Mila carried her tray to a table where Branden and Journey were already seated. Branden grinned and waved her over, while Journey sat hunched over her sketchpad, her pencil cross hatching lines that looked suspiciously like rippling water. Maliyah, meanwhile, drifted toward the older kids.

Zech pulled out a chair at the sixth-graders' table. Andrew sat with his ink-stained hands folded neatly in his lap. Faith hummed under her breath, while Tamia pushed her slipping glasses back up her nose. For a while, the cafeteria buzzed with the normal rhythm of clinking forks and chatter. But then Branden leaned toward Mila, lowering his voice.

"You know the story of the pool, don't you?" Mila froze with her fork halfway to her mouth. "...What story?" Branden smirked. "The Blurred Face Child." Mila shook her head quickly. He leaned closer, his eyes gleaming. "Long ago—back when this was still Blackwood Academy for Boys—there was a kid who wasn't like the others. Didn't have money. Didn't fit in. The school made sure he knew it." Mila's grip on her fork tightened. Branden's voice softened to a near whisper. "They invited him to swim. Made him think he belonged. But when he got to the pool, they dragged him to the deep end. He struggled. Tried to fight. But the water swallowed him."

Mila swallowed hard, her eyes wide. Branden smirked again. "They say the last thing anyone saw was his face... blurring under the ripples as he sank." Across the cafeteria, Zech's voice carried the story forward without missing a beat. "You know why the water's always cold?" he asked Maliyah. "Because he's still down there. Waiting." Maliyah blinked. "...Waiting for what?" Zech leaned forward, resting his elbows on the table. "For someone else to notice him. For someone else to join him."

Faith gasped softly, clutching her hymnal tighter. Tamia rolled her eyes, but her shoulders were tense. Andrew scribbled something into his notebook before looking up. "Some say if you stare at the surface long enough, you'll see him staring back." Maliyah shivered. She thought of the shimmer in the pool, the way the water had seemed to shift with no one near it. By recess, the story had spread its chill through both sisters. The courtyard buzzed with laughter, kids racing to the swings and jungle gym. But somehow, without meaning to, Mila, Maliyah, Branden, Journey, Zech, Andrew, Faith, and Tamia drifted into the same circle near the fountain.

Maliyah spoke first, her voice low. "I think... I saw something today—at the pool." Mila hugged her plush cat against her chest. "Me too." Branden nodded quickly. "That's how it starts. Once you see him, he sees you back." Faith shuddered. "My cousin dreamed of a boy with no face right after swimming in that pool!" Tamia snapped her notebook shut. "Dreams don't mean anything," she muttered. But her eyes flicked toward the gym doors as if daring herself to believe it. Andrew said softly, "Maybe it doesn't matter if it's real. Maybe what matters is that all of us saw... something."

The laughter of the other children seemed far away, the courtyard hushed beneath the heavy shadow of the academy's stone towers. For a moment, none of them spoke. Eight kids, drawn together not by friendship, but by a ghost's unfinished story. After school, the girls arrived early for swim practice. The gymnasium echoed with the hum of the overhead lights.

The pool stretched before them, its surface still—until suddenly, without warning, ripples spread across the water as though someone had just dived in. Maliyah froze.

"Did you see that?" Mila uttered softly. She nodded slowly, her eyes locked on the shifting water. Then she noticed it—wet footprints. They trailed away from the pool, darker against the tile, leading toward the exit. Both girls followed the marks, their sneakers squeaking softly. But just as suddenly as they had appeared, the footprints stopped mid-hallway, vanishing into nothing. Neither spoke for a long moment. It felt wrong, like they had intruded on something not meant for them.

Before the other students arrived, they slipped back inside, choosing not to tell anyone what they had seen—at least not yet. The next day at lunch, the cafeteria was its usual storm of chatter and clattering trays. Mila sat with Branden and Journey, trading pieces of fruit, while Maliyah excused herself, saying she needed a little quiet. She carried her folder and pencil toward the pool, away from the noise, hoping to work on an assignment from her last class. But when she entered the gymnasium, the air felt different—thicker.

She set her folder down on the bench, her eyes drawn to the pool. Something about the water pulled at her, like an invisible thread tugging her forward. Before she could think, she was standing at the edge. The surface shimmered, a dark mirror. She leaned closer. And closer. The next moment, she slipped. The water swallowed her whole, dragging her down in a strange, dreamlike silence. She should have panicked, but

instead, it was as though she were drifting through someone else's memory.

Images swirled around her—the old brick walls of the academy, the harsh bark of a coach's orders, the sharp laughter of boys in old fashioned swimsuits. She saw him. The boy with the blurred face. At first, his features swam in and out of focus, but then, as she drifted deeper, they sharpened into clarity: hollow eyes, a thin frame swimsuit patched at the seams. He stood at the pool's edge, clutching his towel, his classmates circling like predators. "No one wants you here," one sneered.

Another shoved him forward, their laughter echoing cruelly. Maliyah watched helplessly as they threw him into the deep end. His arms flailed, splashing, fighting for air. The water churned violently above his fading face. "No!" she screamed, her voice muffled by the water. She lunged forward, as if she could reach him, pull him back. For a breathless second, she felt his struggle in her own chest. And then—hands grabbed her arms. She broke the surface with a gasp, coughing and thrashing. The gym's harsh lights blinded her until her vision cleared, revealing familiar faces. Mila, Branden, Zech, Faith, Tamia, Journey, even Andrew—they were all there, clustered around the pool, pulling her out. Maliyah collapsed onto the tiles, shivering, her chest heaving for air. "What happened?" Mila cried, clutching her sister's arm. "Why did you fall in?!" "It wasn't—" Maliyah coughed, wiping water from her face. "I didn't fall. I saw him." Her voice shook. "The boy. The blurred-face child. I saw what they did to him." The others exchanged uneasy glances. Zech leaned closer, his voice low.

 "Then it's true," he said. "The story's real." Maliyah nodded, trembling. "And he's still here. He wants us to know what happened to him."

CHAPTER III

The Pact

Above the cafe door, a bell chimed as the group filed in, trailing wet sneakers and nervous glances. The place was dim despite the daylight outside. Its lace curtains drawn halfway, as though trying to keep the sun out. A row of mismatched teapots sat along the shelf, their painted faces chipped and faded. A waitress glided over—thin, tall, her hair pulled so tightly back that it seemed to stretch her smile too wide. "Sit wherever you like, dearies," she said, her voice unsteady, though her eyes flicked past the children to the empty air behind them, as if expecting someone else to follow.

They took a booth near the back. The waitress set down a tray of glasses filled with iced tea and a slice of lemon before the children could even place an order, as though the drinks were already waiting for them, beads of condensation sliding down their sides. "Did we order those?" Mila said in a low voice. "No...," Maliyah murmured. "Don't drink those."

The waitress leaned close to wipe the table, her cloth leaving damp streaks on the wood. "The special today is blueberry pie. Baked fresh this morning." She paused, her voice dropping almost to a whisper. "Don't go near the pool." Before anyone could respond, she straightened, smiling too brightly again. "I'll be back with your pie."

The group sat frozen until she vanished through the kitchen door. "That was..." Branden shifted uneasily, "...creepy, right?" "Understatement," Zech muttered, his skateboard propped beside him. He tapped his fingers on the table. "But she's not wrong. You saw him, Maliyah. The boy's still there. He's stuck."

Journey, who had been silent, finally spoke. Her sketchbook lay open in front of her, the pencil lines forming the outline of the academy's pool. The water shimmered in her drawing like it was alive. "Spirits stay when something holds them. If he's trapped, it means his story hasn't ended."

Mila hugged her plush cat tight. "How do we... help him?" Faith leaned in, lowering her voice as though the walls themselves might be listening. "We need to find out his name. Names are powerful. If we know who he really was, maybe we can... I don't know... help him rest." Zech nodded sharply. "The archives! Blackwood has to keep enrollment records of students from way back. If he drowned, there's got to be something. A headline. A file." "Umm, does anyone else think that's just scary?" Tamia asked, glancing toward the counter where the waitress now stood— still watching them with that same fixed smile. "So creepy."

The group nodded in agreement, each of them slowly turning away, though their eyes continued to flick back toward the counter, checking to see if the waitress was still staring. The conversation quieted. The atmosphere in the café felt heavier. Maliyah finally broke the silence. "I saw his face," she said. "For a moment, I saw him. He wasn't just some blurry shadow. He was a real boy, scared and alone. And if we don't help him... no one will."

Branden leaned back, his usual grin gone. "Then it's up to us." The waitress reappeared, balancing a tray with slices of pie. She set the plates down gently, but as she did, she leaned close enough that Maliyah could smell the faint tang of lemon polish on her apron still holding that unearthly smile. "Enjoy your pie." She said slowly walking away.

When she finally left, the group huddled closer together. "So it's decided," Zech said. "We start digging. Library, records, whatever we can get our hands on. We'll find his name." "And then what?" Mila asked. "Then," Journey said softly, staring at her sketch of the pool, "we set him free."

The bell above the café door chimed again as another customer entered, but the children didn't turn to look. They sat in their booth, their pact sealed in silence, while outside the mist of Greystone pressed tighter against the windows. "Tomorrow, after school, we should all meet at the local library.

Maliyah said, grabbing Mila's hand and pushing their way out the booth. "We can start with the year books." said Journey following behind the girls. Zech slung his skateboard under his arm. "And if the yearbooks don't have it, there's always the old archives. Places like Blackwood don't throw anything away. They just hide it."

The group fell into a tense silence. The waitress was watching them again from the counter, her smile plastered on like a mask. She tapped the bell by the register once, twice, *ding-ding*, as if marking their conversation. They shuffled out into the misty street, the air colder than when they'd gone in. The lampposts flickered even though it wasn't yet evening, and the shadows of the town square seemed to lean closer. As they walked, Branden forced a grin. "So... yearbooks tomorrow. Easy, right? Just dusty old pictures."

"Not always," Zech muttered. "Sometimes pictures show things you weren't supposed to see." Mila clutched her plush cat tight, and though she didn't say it aloud, she couldn't shake the feeling that the waitress was watching them ever so closely-listening to every word they had said.

The children turned down the street toward home, their pact hanging over them like a storm cloud. Tomorrow, they will dig. Tomorrow, they will name him. And from the café window, the waitress watched them vanish into the mist, her hand resting on the glass, her smile fading into something else—something colder.

The next afternoon, the group pushed open the heavy oak doors of Greystone Public Library. The hinges groaned like something alive, and immediately, the air changed. It was colder here, damp and sharp, smelling of mildew and old stone. Dust clung to the walls, turning the paint into something gray and sickly.

Spiderwebs dangled from the corners like lace, and every step they took sent echoes down the hollow aisles. The librarians were somewhat—strange somehow. Their eyes followed the children, their smiles brittle as pressed flowers.

One librarian with hair as white as bone leaned over the counter, whispering to no one as she sorted index cards with shaking hands. Another wheeled a cart of books that squealed and groaned as if protesting every movement. And in the shadows of the reading tables, strange townsfolk lingered—men with hats pulled low, a woman in black gloves who never turned a page.

All of them watching. Always watching. "I hate it here," Mila said in a hush tone, pressing closer to her sister. "Good," Zech said under his breath. "That means we're in the right place." They spread out between the shelves, the scratch of their sneakers the only sound. Minutes stretched long, the silence pressing down, until— "I found something!" Tamia's voice was hushed but urgent.

She pulled a thick yearbook from the shelf, dust puffing into the air like ash. She flipped through brittle pages until she stopped on a sepia-toned photograph. "Here!" Maliyah leaned in, her breath catching. The *swim team*. Rows of boys in outdated swimsuits, their faces proud, their coach rigid at the edge.

And there, near the end of the line, a boy who didn't quite fit. His clothes- a little older, his smile- a little weaker. The others' eyes seemed to glare even through the faded ink. "That's him!" Maliyah said intensely pointing at his image. They pressed on, searching until Journey tugged out a folder of *newspaper* clippings. She spread them on the table. One headline read:

"Local Student Drowns in Academy Pool — Tragic Accident"

The article was short, almost too short. A boy unnamed, his "tragic misstep" brushed aside in a handful of sentences. No photographs. No follow-ups. Just silence. "That can't be all," Faith said, her fingers trembling. "No one dies and just... disappears from history." Andrew's eyes narrowed. "Check the archives."

The basement was a vault of forgotten things—crates of records, locked cabinets, and rows of boxes stacked like tombstones. Dust coated everything, and the buzzing light overhead flickered as though it could barely hold back the dark. Zech pried open one of the boxes. Inside, yellowed papers lay waiting, frail but intact. He handed a folder to Maliyah, and she read the words aloud in a whisper:

"Settlement reached with family—confidential agreement."

She flipped the page. Notes scribbled in the margins told the rest: *bullying... hazing gone too far... pushed into the pool.* But the final page stamped in red said only one thing: **CASE CLOSED**. Mila felt her stomach twist. "They paid them off." "Covered it up," Zech muttered, slamming the folder shut. His face was pale but burning with anger. "They let the boys walk away. No justice. Nothing."

The children stood in silence, the weight of the discovery pressing into their chests. Somewhere above, the building groaned, a sound like something shifting in the walls. "They buried the truth," Maliyah said softly. "And he's still waiting for someone to dig it up."

The group exchanged glances, a silent vow forming between them. This wasn't just a ghost story anymore. It was a secret the whole town had helped to bury. And as they left the archives, one of the mysterious librarians watched them go, her lips curling into the faintest of smiles—like someone who had just seen a door creak open that should have stayed shut.

CHAPTER IV

Whispers in the Halls

The next morning, the children returned to Blackwood Hollow Academy with heavy steps and heavier secrets. They had agreed the night before to say nothing, to keep their discovery buried within their circle. But as soon as they walked through the iron gates, something felt different. The teachers watched them too closely. The custodian paused

while sweeping just to look up and stair. Even the headmistress, usually too busy to notice the younger students, stood at the entrance a moment too long, her gaze following the children as they filed inside.

Maliyah sat stiffly in her English class, pretending to take notes while her mind kept replaying the files they had uncovered. Andrew sat two rows behind, his pencil tapping nervously against his desk. Beside him, Tamia's eyes kept flicking toward the door. Their teacher, Mr. Bellamy, normally droned on without care, but today his pauses were sharper, his gaze unusually intense.

When he placed the worksheet on Maliyah's desk, he didn't say a word—just stared a moment too long, as if he knew what she'd seen. Across the hall in science class, Faith and Zech weren't faring much better. Their teacher, Ms. Harrow, leaned against her desk with her arms folded, her questions oddly pointed. "Some experiments," she said, her eyes sweeping the room, "are better left... untested. Sometimes curiosity leads only to consequences." Faith glanced at Zech, her heart thudding. "That wasn't part of the lesson-right?"

Meanwhile, in the library, Brandon, Mila, and Journey had been assigned to catalog books for a project. The air was thick with dust, the lamps flickering low. Every time Mila reached for a stack, she felt the prickling of eyes. The librarians moved silently between aisles, their hands twitching as they reshelved volumes. One of them stopped beside the children, smoothing her long skirt. "Careful with those books," she said softly, her smile pinched and unnatural. "All stories should be respected."

Mila gulped nervously, clutching her plush snow-cone cat. By the time the bell rang, each group had already decided: they needed to talk. They met at the stairwell between classes, huddling together as students streamed past. "They know," Andrew said glancing around as if to be suspicious of everyone around him. "Every adult in this place…" "Mr. Bellamy kept staring at me," Maliyah leaned in and spoke softly. "Like he was waiting for me to say something." "Ms. Harrow basically threatened us," Faith added, her voice shaky. "And the librarians…"

Mila's voice faltered. "They wouldn't stop watching. It's like they were waiting for us to slip up." The bell rang again, forcing them to scatter. But by lunchtime, the group reconvened on the far edge of the playground, where the fog curled low over the fence and the teachers rarely looked. "Okay," Zech said, lowering his voice. "So we know the school covered it up.

We know they paid the family to keep quiet. The question is—why does everyone still act like theirs more to hide?" "Because there is," Faith said, shivering. "Spirits don't rest when there's no justice." Journey kicked at the dirt. "Then what do we do? Just keep digging? They already know we're looking." It was Tamia who leaned forward, her eyes bright with a dangerous idea. "We don't wait. We don't just read about him. We will go to him."

The others stared at her. "At night," she secretly whispered. "When the halls are empty we'll go back to where it happened—the pool. If his spirit is anywhere, it's there. We sneak back in. We face him. Maybe… maybe that's the only way to help him." The group fell silent. The thought hung between them. "Are you insane?" Brandon shrieked. "That's..." "That's exactly what we have to do," Zech interrupted, his voice hard. "If the adults want us to stay away, it means we're getting close." Maliyah looked around at her friends, at her sister clutching her cat, at the fog pressing against the fence like fingers. Her heart raced, but she nodded. "Tonight," she said. "We go back!"

The night pressed heavy against the windows of the Lynn household. Maliyah lay awake, heart pounding, waiting for the creak of the floorboards to quiet and her parents' voices to fade into silence. Finally, she slipped from her bed, pulling on her hoodie, the moonlight catching the determination in her eyes. Across the hall, Mila was already waiting, holding plush cat against her chest. "Ready?" she asked. Maliyah nodded, squeezing her sister's hand.

Together, they crept down the stairs, careful to avoid the step that always creaked, and slipped out the back door into the mist-soaked night. Their friends were waiting by the rusted gates of the Academy. Zech gave a quick nod. "Everyone made it?" "All here," Tamia confirmed, her voice hushed but steady. The school loomed above them like a sleeping beast. Its stone walls glistened with dampness, the tall windows dark and unwelcoming.

They circled until Andrew found a side door that hadn't latched properly. One by one, they slipped inside, the air colder than it had been outside, smelling faintly of mildew and floor wax. The night janitor's footsteps echoed faintly down the hall. The children pressed themselves against the wall, holding their breath as the beam of his flashlight cut across the corridor before vanishing around the corner. Journey exhaled slowly, "That was close." "Come on," Maliyah said while leading the group down the hall . "Pool's this way." The gymnasium groaned as they pushed open the doors. The pool shimmered beneath the overhead lights, perfectly still, like a mirror.

The bleachers rose in neat rows of shadows, while the faint smell of chlorine hung in the air. Faith broke the silence. "How do we... call him?" Her voice trembled despite her effort to sound brave. Maliyah moved in closer to the pool. "When I saw him... it was because I was in the water." The group exchanged uneasy looks.

One by one, they set down their backpacks and jackets on the bleachers. But Mila hesitated. Her plush cat wasn't just a toy—it was her comfort, her lucky charm when things felt uncertain. Clutching it tightly, she decided to bring it along, telling herself she could always toss it into the dryer afterward when she got home, like a small offering for good luck. Taking a deep breath, she followed the others to the pool's edge, her reflection rippling beside theirs. "Together," Zech said firmly, extending his hand.

They linked fingers, a chain of trembling courage, and on the count of three, they jumped. The splash echoed like thunder in the cavernous gym. The world shifted the moment the water closed over them. The sharp sting of chlorine gave way to a cold, heavy stillness. When they surfaced, gasping, the pool was no longer gleaming under fluorescent lights.

The tiles were cracked, the ceiling beams rotted and dripping. The air smelled of mold and sorrow, unsettling with the weight of time. The bleachers sagged with age, their wood darkened with years of dampness. And there, sitting alone on the middle row of the bleachers, was a boy. His clothes were a century out of place—a striped swimsuit clung to his thin frame. His face, no longer blurred, was pale and gaunt, his eyes hollow with sadness.

The children climbed out of the pool slowly, water dripping down their arms and legs, their shoes squelching on the tile. Even Journey had pulled out glasses that the other children didn't know she had, to see the boy better. They lined up side by side, staring at the boy who stared back at them. For the first time, face to face, they saw the Blurred-Faced Child. His lips trembled as if forming words he hadn't spoken in

years. His gaze lingered on Maliyah, then swept across the others. "You came," he murmured in disbelief.

CHAPTER V

The Names of The Guilty

The pool was no longer bright and modern. The lights had dimmed into a sickly glow, and the air pressed heavy on their lungs. The air clung to them, dense and unyielding. And there — on the splintered bleachers — sat the boy. His face was no longer a blur. Pale skin, wet hair plastered to his forehead, hollow eyes that seemed to have seen too much.

His shoulders sagged under an invisible weight, as though he had been waiting for this moment for decades. The children stood in a crooked line, dripping, shivering, unsure of what to do. It was Andrew who stepped forward first. His voice cracked in the silence.

"M-my name's Andrew... We—" he swallowed hard. "We want to help. May we... may we know yours?" The boy's lips trembled, as if the act of speaking might break him apart. Finally, in a whisper that scraped like old wood, he said: "Thomas. Thomas Avery."

The name seemed to echo across the tiles. Maliyah pressed her fist to her mouth. Her tears came fast, surprising even herself. "Thomas," she said, stumbling closer, "I saw it. I saw what they did to you. I couldn't stop it. I'm so sorry." Her voice cracked, and she sobbed, her shoulders shaking. Thomas's sunken eyes flicked to hers.

For just a moment, his expression softened. "No one ever said that," he mourned, "Not once." Faith wiped her damp hands on her skirt, gathering courage. "How can we help you? How do we set you free?" Tamia leaned forward quickly, desperate, her voice steady despite the tremor in her chin. "You don't belong here, Thomas. You deserve peace. Tell us what we have to do."

Thomas's gaze grew darker. His fingers curled into the fabric of his sweater. "I can't leave. Not while they walk free. Not while the truth rots in silence." A nervous ripple ran through the group. Journey, hugging her arms around herself, found her voice. "Do you... do you blame the boys? The ones who... pushed you in?"

The boy's head dropped. His voice thinned, as though dragged from a place too deep. "They laughed while I drowned. I see their faces still. But laughter dies. One by one, the world swallowed them—fire, illness, a string of 'accidents,' tragedy after tragedy. Time took its due. They are not why I remain." Branden's voice quivered. "What about your parents? Why didn't they—" He couldn't finish.

Thomas's eyes glistened with something more than sorrow. "I don't feel them anymore. Their love is gone from this place. They took the school's money and left my name to drown with me." Mila's said in a small, steady voice, "That must mean... they're gone now. Passed on."

Thomas closed his eyes, jaw tight, as if the truth still hurt after all these years. The children stood silent, their breaths shallow. The air thickened, heavy with his grief. At last, Thomas lifted his chin. "Do you want to know why I remain?" Every child nodded.

And then the story poured out of him. His voice cracked as he described the teasing that never ended, the way the older boys spat the word *pauper* like venom, the sting of being forced to swim until his chest burned, the coach who looked away.

His hands twisted as he relived the night by the pool — the shoving, the water, the helplessness of arms that would not keep him afloat. His voice shook as he spoke of sinking, his face breaking into ripples, the terror of lungs filling with water while laughter carried over the surface. The children listened, rooted in place, some covering their mouths, others clutching each other's hands. Maliyah sobbed openly. Zech trembled so hard his teeth chattered.

Finally, his voice dropped into a cold whisper: "They didn't just drown me. They buried me in silence. The school said I was somewhere I shouldn't be. That I fell. That I hit my head. They paid my parents to disappear. My name was erased." He looked at each of them in turn, hollow eyes meeting theirs. "If you would help me… then speak the names of those who sealed my fate." The air in the pool hall dropped to ice. Thomas's lips barely moved, but the names cut through the silence like knives: "Headmaster Burrow. Dean Woodlock. Miss Angus Crow."

The children gasped. They knew those names. Not well. Not personally. But enough to feel the weight. The water stirred violently at their feet. A rush of air tore through the pool like a scream. "Go," Thomas rasped. "Find them. Expose them. Only then will I be free." A sudden force yanked them backwards. The water swallowed them whole. They kicked and clawed and broke the surface in the present-day pool, gasping for air, chlorine burning their throats.

The tiles gleamed again, the bleachers were new. They scrambled out, dripping, dazed, too shaken to speak. But the names rang in their heads like bells they could not silence. That night, none of them slept. Every time they closed their eyes, they saw the boy's hollow stare, the shimmer of water where he'd once stood. Morning came gray and solemn, the world uncharged—except for them. That day at recess, they huddled beneath their oak, mist swirling like watchful ghosts.

Maliyah spoke softly as though the mist itself might hear: "Headmaster Burrow. Dean Woodlock. Miss Angus Crow."

Faith hugged her arms. "I swear… They were watching us yesterday. In class. In the halls. They know we know." Zech's voice was tight. "Then we watch them and we find out what they're hiding." "Split up," Journey said. "Groups of three's and two. Each one of us takes a name. Then we'll come back together." They nodded, solemn. Zech and Faith claimed Burrow.

Maliyah, Tamia, and Andrew would take Woodlock.

Journey, Mila, and Branden would face Miss Crow. The bell rang, but none of them moved. Their pact had been sealed. From the school's stone steps, a tall figure paused, watching. Miss Crow's silhouette stretched long across the mist. Beside her, the headmaster's shadow shifted, one hand brushing his pocket as though guarding something.

The children pretended not to see. But in their bones, they knew—the game had started and the investigations began. Zech and Faith trailed Headmaster Burrow down the long stone hallway.

His shoes clicked like a metronome, his posture rigid. They ducked behind columns, careful not to be seen. Burrow paused at his office door, glancing over his shoulder as though he felt eyes. Then he slipped inside.

Through the crack, Faith caught a glimpse — rows of old ledgers stacked on shelves and a locked cabinet that Burrow stood by, key turning with a sharp *click*. "Secrets," Zech said confidently. "I bet the truth is in there." Meanwhile, Maliyah,

Tamia, and Andrew lingered near Dean Woodlock's classroom.

The dean was notorious for his sharp tongue, his dislike for anyone who asked too many questions. When the last student left, the trio slipped inside. The room smelled of pipe smoke and chalk. Papers littered his desk, neat at first glance, but Andrew quickly found one sheet tucked beneath the rest. A faded letterhead, stamped with the academy's crest. "'Compensation agreement... Avery family,'" Tamia read aloud in a whisper.

Her heart hammered. "This is the proof, exactly what we're looking for." Maliyah's face sank. "This is so sad, how could they" Across the building, Journey, Mila, and Branden sat through music class with Miss Crow. Her bony fingers clutched the baton as she conducted.

A silver whistle hung on a chain at her throat—not for gym, but because she doubled as Blackwood's Safety Marshal and a choir director; one sharp blast could call drills or cue entrances in the courtyard. Her eyes — cold and sharp — kept straying to the children as though she could see inside their heads. Mila shivered.

When the lesson ended, they lingered behind. Journey nudged Branden toward the back office. There, among stacks of hymnals, lay a box half-hidden beneath a cloth. Inside were photographs. A swim team lineup. Boys in striped swimsuits. And there, at the edge, Thomas Avery, eyes wide and uncertain.

And scribbled on the front:

"*Expunge. Do not circulate.*"

The sound of heels clicking made them slam the box shut. Miss Crow's shadow filled the doorway. "Children," she said alarmingly suspcious. "Run along." Her eyes lingered too long. That night, the children met again in secret. They pieced together what they'd seen: the locked cabinet, the compensation papers, the suppressed photographs. Every clue pointed to one thing — the truth about Thomas Avery had been silenced by them. Maliyah clenched her fists. "Then we won't be silent. Not anymore." The mist pressed tighter around them, as though the town itself was listening.

CHAPTER VI

The Truth Set Free

That night, the Greystone Public Library felt colder than usual. Shadows crept along the corners, and the dusty air made the lamplight look dull and gray. On one of the old shelves sat a damaged yearbook. Inside, the school's swim team stared out from a faded photo—some smiling, others caught mid-laugh, towels tossed over their shoulders.

On the bottom row was a boy partly hidden behind a towel: Thomas Avery. Above his head, neat letters spelled out the names of the adults in charge-Burrow, Headmaster. Woodlock, Dean. Crow, Secretary to the Headmaster.

"If the school won't tell his story," Mila raised her head tall, voice shaking but sure, "we will."

"The Investigators," Zech said, grim and bright. "Let's publish this!" The night pressed close against the Lynn household windows. Hoodies zipped. Sneakers laced tight. The back door creaked open to a cool hush that swallowed their words. Their friends waited near Blackwood's rusted gate—figures barely visible beneath the flicker of a distant streetlight. Andrew led the way to the same side door he'd found before, still unlocked.

Inside, the hallway stretched long and silent, every step echoing as they crept toward the faint hum of the copier. They had just fed the first sheet when the corridor went dark and three silhouettes filled the doorway—Burrow with a wolf-quiet voice, Woodlock tapping his cane like a clock you couldn't outrun, and Miss Crow smiling as if the expression had been sewn on.

"You mistake curiosity for courage," Burrow said, stepping over the threshold as portraits along the corridor turned their heads to listen. "Blackwood is older than your outrage."
"We kept this quiet to protect futures—yours included," Woodlock rasped.
Crow's silver whistle chimed once—delicate, deadly. "Put the papers down children, and this ends."

Maliyah lifted the compensation letter, hands shaking but steady. "Is it necessary to drown a boy twice? First in water, then in silence?" Andrew read the margin notes aloud—pushed... hazing... payment—and Crow lunged, but Zech kicked his board into a rolling cart, metal shrieking as it toppled between them.

The ceiling groaned; wet footprints unfurled toward the gym. From the cold draft, a small voice rose, "Say my name!" They ran for the pool and the school ran with them—stairs lengthening, exit signs blinking out like dying fireflies.

The gym doors flew inward as if yanked by invisible hands, and the water rose in a glassy swell that shaped a boy's face for a heartbeat. Burrow's calm shattered. "Publish this and you'll scorch the town—donors, parents, your own families."

"Then let it burn clean," Journey said, clutching the photographs.

Woodlock's cane struck the tiles—once, twice, three times. The sound cracked through the air like thunder. The pool's lane lines snapped tight, thrashing beneath the surface as if something deep below had awakened.

Crow stumbled backward, shouting orders no one could hear. The lights flickered, and the air seemed to tremble. Thomas Avery was there. His presence rippled through the air, unseen yet furious, bending the water to his will.

The pool erupted in a spiraling wave that tore across the deck, sweeping past the children as if shielding them and crashing toward. The men who had wronged him. Burrow slipped, crashing into the wall as the swirling water struck the tiles, sending Crow's key ring skittering into the shallow end.

Branden pushed open the fire door and called out, "I've got it —this way!" The echo of his voice carried through the chaos as the other ran toward the door. Maliyah, stop!" someone called, she froze mid-step. Slowly she turned, remembering what Thomas Avery had asked of them—what he needed to be free. Drawing a deep breath, she lifted her voice so everyone could hear. **"Thomas Avery!"** Maliyah said clearly, the name ringing like a bell. The swell bowed, almost grateful. *"Run,"* the draft whispered again. They burst into the night, papers pressed beneath their coats, the tower tolling the wrong hour behind them.

By morning, whispers slid through Blackwood like drafts under a door. The headmaster never came to unlock his office; Dean Woodlock's cane was found propped beside the gym doors. Miss Crow's whistle lay caught in the pool's floor grate, a thin ribbon of rust threading the water. The locked cabinet in Burrow's office hung open as if pried from the inside; portraits along the corridor had turned themselves to face the wall.

Custodians followed three sets of wet footprints to the pool's edge—and nowhere back. No one saw Burrow, Woodlock, or Crow again, and the children would never truly know what happened in the hours after they ran. Some say the air inside the pool room turned cold, carrying the sharp scent of old pennies and rain. The water began to climb the tiles, slow and steady, as if answering into the dark.

Woodlock's can struck twice, then vanished beneath the rippling surface, spinning until it was gone Crow's whistle gave one final note before the water swallowed it whole. When the echoes faded, the pool stilled, the lane lines straightened themselves like nothing had ever happened.

No one ever found Woodlock, Burrow, or Crow. Students say their names were wiped from the school records overnight. Others whisper that, on quiet evenings, you can still hear the faint tap of a cane or the soft ring of a whistle beneath the water's surface. But the truth—whatever it was—sank with them that night thus becoming another eerie legend of Blackwood Hollow Academy.

Their first issue of **The Investigators** spread faster than a rumor—slipped beneath desks, passed under cafeteria tables, slid across kitchen counters with coffee rings blooming on the corners. By the weekend, the local paper picked it up. Whispers flared to anger; anger to protest. Families gathered at the gates, demanding justice for the boy their town had tried to forget. In the end, the school bowed. A plaque rose on the pool room wall: **Thomas Avery Hall** *"May his memory never be silenced again."*

That night, the children returned to the water. The air was thick with mist; the surface lay black as glass.

"Ready?" Maliyah asked.

Hands linked. They jumped. Light poured through windows that weren't there before. The water gleamed like a blessing. Thomas stood at the edge—whole now, bright now, eyes like morning.

"Thank you," he said, voice clear as a hymn.

"Swim with us?" Maliyah asked, laughing through tears. "One last time—as our friend."

"I'd like that," he smiled. They cannon balled together into the shining water. For a heartbeat—pure joy. When they surfaced, the light was gone; the pool was just a pool. But the plaque on the wall glowed faintly, warm as gratitude. Thomas Avery was free. And because of them, he would never be forgotten.

CHAPTER VII

The Haunting of the Twin Pranksters

Night air shimmered with fog as the children drifted away from the Academy grounds. They walked close together, their laughter thin and uncertain—like the last notes of a fading song. The echo of Thomas Avery's farewell lingered in their minds, restless as a half-remembered dream. Greystone lay still beneath a lid of mist.

Streetlamps hummed and flickered; old shop signs swayed on their hinges in a wind that didn't seem to touch the children at all. Maliyah kept glancing over her shoulder toward the distant silhouette of Blackwood Hollow. Against the clouds, it looked almost peaceful now—*almost*.

"Do you think he's really gone?" Journey asked, clutching her sketchbook close. "He's free," Maliyah said softly. "I could feel it." Mila thought to herself without saying a word, "Then why does it still feel like something's following us?" The mist thickened, curling around their legs as they turned down the narrow lane toward Elm Row. Ahead, the twins' home stood between a line of old houses built shoulder-to-shoulder, each window dark and watchful.

Everyone at the Academy knew Elijah and Elias Grant—Greystone's legendary pranksters. Their tricks were infamous: false fire alarms, chalk-drawn phantoms, lockers that howled when opened. But lately, even their laughter had changed. It had lost its warmth, stretched thin, and brittle—like laughter that had forgotten what it meant to be human.

Zech kicked a pebble into the fog. "Bet they're plotting something again," he muttered. "They always are." As if on cue, a pale flash flared behind the curtain of the twins' house—cold, white, and unnatural. The group froze.

Inside, something clattered—a frame slipping from the wall. Then silence. A long, scraping noise followed, deliberate and heavy, like iron dragged across wood. A moment later, the upstairs window shimmered with another flicker of light, faint but steady, casting a sickly glow across the front porch. "Maybe they're testing a prank," Branden suggested, though his voice wavered. "Then where's the laughter?" Tamia asked, pushing her glasses higher on her nose.

The lights blinked out. The fog pressed tighter around them. Then came the sound—soft giggles at first, rising, twisting, splitting into two voices that tangled and clashed. The laughter warped—childlike one moment, sharp and hollow the next—until it cracked, no longer sounding human at all. Mila's voice trembled. "Maliyah... look." The upstairs window, a handprint bloomed against the glass—wet, trembling, freshly pressed from the inside. Another appeared beside it, a perfect twin. Both began to slide downward in slow, streaking trails before vanishing completely.

No one moved. "I think we should go," Tamia whispered. But Maliyah couldn't move. The house seemed to breathe—the walls flexing, the curtains shifting as if inhaling. Behind the window, two faint figures stood side by side. The fog thickened.

The laughter deepened—rattling, broken by a jagged intake of breath, the kind that curls just before a scream. And then, from somewhere between the front steps and the doorway, a voice rasped— **"Found you."** The porch lights flickered once... twice... Then the entire street went black.

The darkness felt alive—thick, listening. Even the wind seemed to hold its breath. Somewhere in the fog, a single laugh—sharp and distant—rose and dissolved. Zech swallowed hard. "Yeah," he murmured, agreeing with Tamia's trembling voice, "let's just go." They stepped back together, each footfall measured, careful, until the twins' home disappeared behind the veil of mist.

The town's lights shimmered faintly through the haze like a row of dying candles, and not one of them spoke again until the main street came into view. That night, something about home felt different.

The Lynn house had always been filled with sound—Kylo's low bark, the creak of floorboards, the shuffle of slippers on wood but tonight, every noise carried an echo that didn't belong. When Maliyah bent to grab her backpack, a high-pitched squeak came from under her foot. She jumped. "What the...?" Mila peeked over her blanket, "That wasn't me." Maliyah frowned. "Then who…?" A loud *pfffft!* broke the tension. Mila gasped, then burst out laughing. "Okay, seriously—did you do that?" "I thought you did!"

They tore the bed apart until they found it—a tiny whoopee cushion tucked under the blanket. Maliyah turned it over, baffled. "How did this even…" She stopped short. Another cushion sat perfectly centered on her desk chair, puffed and waiting.

The sisters exchanged uneasy glances. "Maybe… someone's just playing around?" Mila said in such an unsure small voice. But when Maliyah turned out the lamp and climbed into bed, she could swear she heard soft laughter drifting through the dark—two voices, faint and overlapping, coming from the corner of the room.

By lunchtime the next day at school, the group gathered near the courtyard fountain, watching chaos unfold across the grounds. Across the courtyard, the Grant twins sat next to the outdoor lockers to eat lunch, trying to pretend everything was normal. Elijah reached for his sandwich just as the locker behind him flung open and smacked him squarely on the back of the head.

Elias burst out laughing, but before he could finish, his tray vanished—then reappeared upside down, splattering soup across his shoes. Faith's brow furrowed. "Tell me you're seeing this too." Maliyah nodded slowly. "Yeah. We are definitely seeing what you're seeing." The courtyard roared with laughter. But the twins didn't join in. Elias looked around, "Elijah… that wasn't you, right?" His brother shook his head, silent.

The others exchanged quick, nervous glances. When the bell finally rang, no one rushed off. The group lingered by the fountain, tension clinging to the air like static. "That wasn't some prank," Andrew said, gripping his notebook. "That tray *moved*!" "Yeah," Zech added. "And the locker thing?" Tamia crossed her arms.

"Looks like they're being haunted." Branden smirked. "Haunted? By who—each other?"
Faith's voice lowered. "No. By something else." Before anyone could respond, two voices called from behind. Elijah and Elias stood there, no trace of their usual mischief.

They looked exhausted—haunted in the truest sense. "Hey," Elijah started, rubbing the back of his neck. "You guys were there last night, right? You saw our house?" Maliyah nodded. "We did." Elias's voice trembled. "Then maybe you'll believe us when we say something's wrong." Zech frowned. "Wrong how?" Elijah exhaled. "Since you left, our house hasn't stopped. Doors slamming. Lights flickering. Our alarm clock went off at 3:33 a.m. with *someone* laughing through the speakers." Faith blinked hard. "Laughing?"

"Yeah," Elias said quietly. "But it wasn't us." The group stood silent as the fountain burbled between them, the water rippling with each unsettled breath. Finally, Maliyah spoke. "Meet us after school. At your home. We'll let our parents know we are having a study group there and we can get this all figured out."

The twins hesitated, then nodded. As they turned away, the wind swept through the courtyard, carrying faint, distorted laughter that faded into nothing. For just an instant, Maliyah stared into the water's reflection. Two shadowy boys grinned back at her—thin smiles stretching wider before the ripples erased them. A chill swept across the courtyard. That night, chaos returned. When the group arrived, the twins' home looked just like any other on the street—inviting, ordinary, almost comforting.

The faint glow of the living room spilled across the floor, and the television hummed softly with the sound of cartoons, cheerful voices echoing through the hall. For a fleeting moment, it felt like a place built for laughter, for birthdays and sleepovers, for the kind of childhood memories that should never turn dark.

But beneath that comfort, something subtle pulsed—like the house itself was listening. The cartoons stuttered mid-laugh, the air shifted ever so slightly, and a chill crept in from nowhere at all. Then, without warning— Every door inside the twins' home slammed in succession—each one striking like a thunderclap that rattled the glass panes. Light bulbs sputtered, dimmed, then flickered to life in a jaundiced glow that made the wallpaper look sickly. The air thickened, metallic and cold.

Then, from the far wall, came a sound that didn't belong. A giggle. The family photographs—rows of smiling faces—had begun to move. Their eyes gleamed like wet stones, their mouths twisting wider until the painted teeth seemed to tremble with laughter. The giggling multiplied, rolling through the frames like an echo trying to find its voice. Elias stumbled back, his breath ragged. "It's happening again"

"Why?" Elijah's words came out in a shudder. "Why *us*?" THUD!

A heavy step on the staircase. Another. Every head turned toward the sound. Two pale figures appeared halfway down—the same height, the same outline as the twins—but translucent, as though trapped behind a pane of moving fog. Their faces were smeared with distortion, features melting and reforming with each flicker of light. And then, softly—high and sing-song—their voices drifted through the hall: "Gooooot youuuu..."

The melody wasn't loud, but it slithered beneath the skin, thin and cold. The air itself seemed to hum along. All around them, the twins' prank toys stirred to life—rubber snakes writhing across the carpet, fake spiders spinning from invisible threads, whoopee cushions inflating and deflating with ghostly laughter. Marbles rolled from nowhere, circling the twins' feet in dizzying spirals. Faith's voice cracked. "They're... playing."

Maliyah's eyes narrowed. "No. They're *mocking* us." The voices rose again, drawn-out and sing-song: "Knooock... knoooock..." The house froze. Then, from the far corner, the same eerie tone answered back—off-key, childish: "Whooo's theeeere...?"

The sound warped, stretching too long, too cheerful to be real. The room held its breath. Then both figures leaned forward, smiling wider than any face should, and crooned together— "Your turn." Every toy stopped. The giggling died. The lights steadied. Silence.

Then, with a slow groan, the front door eased open. For a moment, everyone stood still. Then Branden shouted, "Run!" They bolted—feet pounding the floor.

They spilled into the night. The cold wind bit at their skin as they gathered beneath a streetlamp, its light fluttering like a heartbeat. Faith sank to her knees, panting. "Is everyone… okay?" Zech leaned forward, still catching his breath. "I think so." Maliyah pulled Mila close, forcing a steady tone. "We're fine."

No one spoke for awhile as they all tried to catch their breathes. Only the flickering light filled the space between them. Then Zech turned toward the twins, his voice low. "Where are your parents right now?" Elias rubbed his head with his sleeve. "It's date night. They went to the movies." Zech exhaled through his teeth. "Then you two aren't staying here tonight. You're coming to my place. At least till we figure this out." The twins looked at each other, hesitant but clearly relieved. Just then, Andrew straightened, his eyes locked on the house across the street. The windows were still—dark, unmoving—but they carried a weight that felt aware. Watching.

He took one slow step forward, his tone calm but sure. "I guess," he said quietly, " It's our turn now." The others followed his gaze. The fog thickened, until only the faint outline of the house remained. Then somewhere deep within that shifting mist—a small, crooked laugh rippled through the night.

And just like that, Greystone fell silent again. By the next morning, Greystone's fog had thinned, leaving the courtyard at Blackwood Hollow Academy sparkling under a pale stretch of sunlight. For once, the Investigators weren't whispering about hauntings or running from shadows — they were laughing. "Okay, okay—but the sound it made!" Zech said, gasping between fits of laughter. "I swear the whole bench jumped!"

Mila's face went crimson. "How was I supposed to know someone left a whoopee cushion there?" Journey nearly dropped her sketchbook from laughing. "You said, *See? Totally safe!*' right before you sat down!" Branden clutched his stomach. "The face you made—oh man, I can't breathe!"

Even Faith's laugh rang out across the courtyard. "If any ghosts were after us, that noise sure would've scared them off." Tamia held up her phone. "I got the whole thing on video." "You didn't!" Maliyah gasped, lunging for her.

"Oh, I did." The courtyard erupted again as everyone chased Tamia in circles, their laughter echoing off the school walls. For a few moments, it was the kind of joy that chased away the fog; the kind they hadn't felt in weeks. Then Zech glanced past them and spotted two familiar figures walking across the yard. Elijah and Elias Grant. The twins looked refreshed — bright-eyed, their hair still messy but faces lighter than before.

"Hey, guys!" Zech called. "How are you doing today?" "Better," Elijah said with a grin. "Finally got some sleep. Thanks again for letting us crash at your place. And tell your mom her pancakes were *legendary*." Zech laughed. "You're welcome anytime. I'm pretty sure she made enough batter to feed an entire Marine base." Branden elbowed Elias. "So, no more spooky noises?" Elias hesitated, a half-smile tugging at his mouth. "Not last night. But... this morning's been weird."

Faith looked up. "Weird how?" Elijah scratched his head. "Locker slamming, whispers. The broom closet door opened on its own." Maliyah's smile faded. "Still happening?" The twins exchanged a look. Elias nodded slowly. "Yeah. And I think we know why." The group fell quiet. Even the laughter lingering in the air seemed to die down.

Elijah took a deep breath. "It started at Cedar Hollow Café." He stared at the ground, words coming out carefully. "We thought we'd pull one last prank before the end of the week. Something wild — not mean, just funny, something the whole town would talk about, not just the kids at school. The café ladies always scolded us for hanging around after school, so... we hid out after closing. Waited until they turned off the lights." Elias took over. "We found the kitchen door locked, so we—uh—used a butter knife to jimmy it open. It wasn't even hard. But inside..." He paused, frowning. "It looked like a storage room — old, dusty — and it smelled like burnt herbs and something sweet." Elijah nodded. "There were jars everywhere. Not labeled 'sugar' or 'flour' or anything normal; they had things in them. Weird things. Dried frogs. Tiny bones. Bats. Even a porcupine quill." Faith's brow furrowed. "You found a witch's room." "Maybe," Elijah said softly. "We didn't believe it, though. We thought it was for Halloween decorations or something. Then we saw this book sitting on a shelf. Black leather, old, with symbols carved into it. Looked like something out of a movie." Elias swallowed.

"I reached for it. A few jars broke when we bumped the shelf — the air filled with that same sweet, burnt smell. We tried to catch the book before it hit the floor, but it ripped open. A page tore out." "And you put it back?" Zech asked carefully. Elijah's silence was answer enough. "We... took it," Elias admitted quietly.

"We thought it was a recipe or something. But after that night... things started happening at our house." Elijah nodded, "Our bedroom lights flicked on and off all night. The kitchen chairs were upside down when we woke up. And our dog—he wouldn't go near our room anymore. He just stood in the hallway and growled." Elias agreed "That's when we knew... that page we took—needs to go back!"

He looked up, eyes uncertain. "We never told anyone." Faith's voice was quiet. "And that's when it started following you." Elijah nodded. "Not just that. We made another mistake." Maliyah frowned. "There's more?" Elias' voice was heavy. "The library."

The others waited. He continued, "We wanted to pull a prank for the school's documentary contest. Something dramatic. We decided to film a fake haunting at Greystone Public Library. The librarians there always gave us grief for sneaking into the archive room, so... we figured we'd make them the stars."

Branden frowned. "How'd you pull that off?" Elijah sighed. "We brought fishing wire, pulleys — the whole setup. We hung it behind the portrait of Mrs. Heyward — the founder of the library. The plan was for the picture to 'float' off the wall while we filmed it, make it look haunted." Faith's eyes widened. "That portrait's a hundred years old."

Elias nodded miserably. "Yeah. We didn't know the wire would snap. The frame came down hard and missed Mrs. Danton by maybe two inches. She screamed. We thought she was angry, but she didn't say a word. She just picked up the picture, set it back, and whispered something." "What did she say?" Maliyah asked softly.

Elijah's voice was barely a whisper. "She said, '*Some laughter earns its echo.*' And then she walked away." The group sat in stunned silence. Faith finally spoke. "Then it's not over until you put back what you took." Elias looked uneasy. "The page?" She nodded. "Whatever was written on that page belongs to that room. Until it's back where it came from, you'll never be left alone." Maliyah straightened, resolve in her eyes. "Then we start where it began." "The café," Faith said.

Tamia crossed her arms. "After school?" "After school," Faith confirmed. The twins exchanged a nervous look, but Elijah managed a small grin. "If we make it back alive, I'll never pull a prank again."

And just as the bell rang, a faint squeak echoed from under the bench. Mila froze. Everyone turned. She sighed, mortified. "Oh, come on!" The courtyard erupted in laughter again

— loud, genuine, unguarded. But somewhere beneath that laughter, almost buried in the sound, came another faint echo. A giggle.

Not theirs.

And it didn't fade when the laughter stopped.

CHAPTER VIII

The Return to Cedar Hollow Cafe

By late afternoon, the fog had lifted completely, and for once Greystone looked like any other small town — quiet, sunlit, harmless. Maliyah and Mila walked home together, backpacks bouncing against their shoulders. As soon as they stepped through the door, the smell of dinner — garlic bread and roasted chicken — filled the air.

Their mom looked up from the kitchen island and smiled. "Hey, girls! How was school?" Maliyah dropped her bag. "Good. Long, but good." Dad peeked around the corner, wiping his hands on a dish towel. "You two settling in okay? Making friends?" Mila beamed. "We're winning!"

Dad raised an eyebrow. "Winning at what, sweetheart?" "Fighting ghosts," Mila said proudly. "And hauntings." She leaned closer, lowering her voice dramatically. "We're winning." Mom blinked, then chuckled. "Oh, really?"

"Yep! The twins were cursed, but we're helping." Maliyah froze mid-step, staring at her sister like *please stop talking right now.* Mom smiled, amused. "Well, that sounds... exciting. You sure you're not reading too many spooky books before bed?" "It's true!" Mila said, hands on her hips. Maliyah laughed nervously and started nudging her toward the door. "Okay! We'll, uh, finish the story later! We promised the group we'd meet up for hot chocolate at the café." Dad smiled. "The one downtown?" "Yeah, Cedar Hollow."

He nodded approvingly. "That sounds nice. Just stay where there's light and people, okay?" "Got it!" Maliyah said, already ushering her sister toward the hall. Mila looked over her shoulder, grinning. "Don't worry, Mom. If ghosts show up, we got this." Mom laughed. "You and your imagination!"

As the door closed behind them, Maliyah sighed and whispered, "Mila, you can't tell them that!" Mila shrugged, giggling. "What? They thought it was cute." Maliyah shook her head but smiled. "You're gonna get us grounded *and* ghosted."

Across the Street from Cedar Hollow Café By dusk, the group had gathered again — Zech, Tamia, Branden, Faith, the twins, Journey and the sisters. The café glowed warm from the inside, its striped awning fluttering in the wind. Through the front windows, the waitresses moved calmly, serving coffee and pie to the evening crowd. Branden asked, "Are we really doing this?"

Faith's eyes stayed on the building. "I don't think we have a choice." Maliyah crossed her arms. "So what's the plan?" Elijah pulled the folded page from his pocket, still slightly burnt at the edges. "We put this back where it came from. Quietly. Tonight." Elias nodded. "We'll just go in like normal, act casual, see if that room's still sealed." Andrew — always the tinkerer — adjusted his backpack strap. "I brought a hammer. If the door's still nailed shut, I can handle it." Tamia patted her jacket pocket. "And I brought a picklock. Just in case they went overboard on the locks." Faith gave a small approving nod. "Good. We'll split up once we're inside. One group orders food, the other looks for a way back into that room." Mila tugged on her sister's sleeve. "What do we do?" Maliyah smiled softly. "We stay close and look innocent."

Inside the Café

The bell above the door jingled as they entered. The café was warm, cozy, crowded enough that their nerves faded just a bit. They ordered drinks and found a booth in the corner. Elijah scanned the room carefully as they took their seats. "There's the back door to the kitchen." They all noticed it at once.

Journey leaned in whispered a plan— to split into pairs and look for any doors or windows that might still be open after the café closed. A few minutes later, Tamia slipped quietly from the booth, pretending to check her phone. She returned a minute later, whispering, "The bathroom's window is open just enough for us to squeeze through." "No cameras?" Faith asked."Didn't see any." Answered Tamia Elijah nodded. "Then that's our way in." They finished their drinks, smiled politely at the waitresses, and left just before closing — the plan set.

Midnight

The streets of Greystone were empty. Streetlamps buzzed. One by one, the kids reappeared from the shadows near the alley beside the café. Faith whispered, "Everyone got what they need?" Andrew lifted his backpack. "Hammer, flashlight, snacks. We're good." Tamia cracked her knuckles. "Let's do this before I lose my nerve." They boosted one another through the open bathroom window. The window slammed shut behind them with a sharp *bang*.

The sound bounced off the tiled walls, making every child flinch. For a long second no one moved. Only the steady drip of a leaking faucet broke the silence. Inside, the café looked different — colder, heavier, the air thick with that same burnt-sweet scent and an uneasy silence that was soon cut with the eerie sound of humming. Low. Slow. Ancient. Maliyah crouched beside Mila behind a booth. "Stay down," she whispered. Zech and the twins slid behind the counter, Faith and Tamia near the pastry case.

Each heart beat loud enough to give them away. The humming grew louder — more voices joining, like a hundred whispers layered together. The kitchen door creaked open, spilling golden light across the wet floor. From the glow appeared three figures. The first, an older woman with long silver hair and paper-thin skin — glided forward clutching two heavy books to her chest.

Her eyes burned faintly red, and her grin stretched far too wide, carved into her face like a scar. The second, thin as a matchstick, wearing the café's tan apron, moved beside her, water dripping from her fingers. Her smile trembled, fixed and unnatural, her eyes wide and hollow like glass marbles. Behind them, half in shadow, lingered a third, tall, pale, her face flickering in and out of the candlelight, lips moving silently with the others' hum. They weren't walking.

They were *floating* — inches above the floor, skirts and aprons swaying though the air was still. Mila's eyes widened. She held her face into her plush cat tight. The witches drifted deeper into the room, heads turning sharply, scanning between tables and booths, the hum never breaking. The golden light from the kitchen followed them like smoke. Elias tried not to breathe.

His fingers clenched the folded page in his pocket. The parchment felt hot. Faith met Maliyah's eyes from across the room and mouthed, *Now what?* Maliyah could only shake her head. Then — a creak. One of the witches twisted her neck toward the sound, the motion sharp, birdlike. The hum stopped. The silence that followed was worse. In the back corner, Branden and Journey crouched beneath the dessert counter. Steam curled from the coffee machine above them. Journey's whisper barely rose above the dripping. "They're going to find us."

Branden's eyes darted upward. Overhead, the red handle of the fire alarm glinted faintly in the strobe of the candles. He leaned closer. "If we set it off..." Journey nodded. No words needed. They counted together, mouths forming the numbers silently.

Three...Two...One.

Branden reached up and yanked. The alarm shrieked — a violent, mechanical scream that filled the café. A second later, icy water burst from the ceiling. The witches' reaction was instant. Their glowing eyes flared white, and a collective scream erupted from their throats — a sound that wasn't human.

Steam hissed where the water touched them, filling the café with fog. Candles burst, light splintered, and the hum turned to a roar. "RUN!" Zech shouted, twisting the front-door lock with both hands. The latch gave. The door flew open, and cold night air rushed in. The group bolted out onto the wet pavement, slipping and sliding, shoving one another toward the street.

Inside, the witches convulsed beneath the sprinklers, voices overlapping, shouting in words the kids couldn't understand. "PROTECT THE BOOK! PROTECT THE BOOK!"

Branden stumbled outside, laughing breathlessly through his terror. "Guess not all witches melt in water!"

Journey smacked his arm, grinning despite herself. "Shut up and keep running!" They dashed across the street, drenched and shaking, the alarm wailing behind them. When they finally stopped, panting in the shadows of the opposite sidewalk, Mila turned — and froze. Through the café window stood the witches. Three of them. Soaked. Perfectly still.

Their wet clothes clung to their bodies, and their eyes glowed faintly behind the glass. The tallest one held the blackened book against her chest, its cover still steaming. All three smiled. Long. Wide. Wrong. Maliyah whispered, "I think we better start running." No one argued. They turned and fled into the night, leaving the glowing café behind and the eyes that followed them until they vanished around the corner.

CHAPTER IX

The Weekend of Tricks

Saturday morning arrived unusually clear for Greystone. The fog that usually wrapped around the coast had vanished overnight, leaving the air bright, crisp, and filled with the smell of salt and seaweed. The ocean wind rustled through the narrow streets, and seagulls cried above the rooftops. It should have been peaceful. It wasn't.

Maliyah and Mila

Maliyah was helping her mom load laundry when the washing machine clicked on by itself. Mom frowned, pressing the off button. "That's strange." The machine stopped. Then it started again. Click. The water surged. Mom sighed. "This thing's possessed." She turned it off again but the dryer beside it

beeped twice, then started spinning on its own. Mila peeked around the corner, wide-eyed. "Mom?" Before anyone could speak, the living room TV flicked on from down the hall — static buzzing, then a faint laugh echoing through the house. Mom shook her head, exasperated. "We must be having an electrical short. Maliyah, unplug that TV." Maliyah's voice was barely a whisper. "It's them."

Zech

Zech was in his driveway shooting hoops, earbuds in, humming along to his playlist. The first two shots swished perfectly. On the third, the ball hit the rim, bounced up— and *exploded*. Bright orange confetti rained down over him. Zech froze, jaw dropping. Then a faint giggle drifted through the still air. "Okay," he said, hands raised, backing toward the door, "game over. I'm retired."

Faith

Faith liked quiet Saturdays. She'd already made her bed, lined up her notebooks, and was reorganizing her bookshelf when her mom called from downstairs. "Faith! Did you leave the water running?" "No!" she answered. She turned to grab a pen, and when she looked back, her perfectly made bed was messy — the blankets tangled and hanging halfway off. Faith blinked. "What in the..." She fixed it again, tight corners, neat folds.

Then stepped into the hallway. A second later she peeked back inside. Her comforter was gone. "...You've got to be kidding me." She found it in the hallway, neatly folded — and sitting upright like someone had placed it there to wait. Faith backed away slowly. "Nope. Absolutely not. Not today."

Branden and Journey

Journey's living room was lit only by the glow of the TV screen. She and Branden sat cross-legged on the carpet, controllers in hand. "Alright," Branden said, grinning. "You're going down this time." "Please," Journey said. "You couldn't beat me if you had cheat codes." The countdown finished. 3... 2... 1... FIGHT! Their characters lunged forward — and immediately began... dancing. Branden frowned. "What—what's happening?" Onscreen, the two warriors

twirled gracefully, doing a waltz instead of swinging their swords. Journey started laughing until both characters turned toward the screen, their pixelated faces grinning too wide, eyes glowing bright white.

Then the game froze. The speakers let out a faint hum. Journey whispered, "Turn it off."

"I'm trying," Branden said, mashing buttons. The console clicked off by itself. They sat there in silence, hearts pounding. Branden said apprehensively "We're going back to the café, aren't we?" Journey nodded. "Oh yeah."

Tamia

Tamia was lounging on her bed, re-watching her whoopee-cushion video for the tenth time. "Classic," she said, grinning. But halfway through, the laughter stopped. The sound warped — Mila's startled squeak stretched, deepened, and turned into a blood-curdling scream. The room went silent. Tamia stared at the screen. "Nope." She hit delete. The video vanished. A moment later, her phone camera turned on by itself, pointing straight at her face. She dropped it. "Definitely nope."

Andrew

Andrew was relaxing on the couch. At the end of the couch where his head was laying sat an old wooden end table. On the table, a phone rested in its cradle — silent, ordinary, harmless. The phone rang once. ⬦Then twice. He ignored it at first, figuring someone else in the house would get it. But when it rang a third time, the sound felt closer, more insistent — almost like it was calling *for him*. With a sigh, Andrew reached over and picked up the receiver. "Hello?" Nothing — just a faint hum through static. The sound wavered in and out, like someone humming a tune from underwater. It was so quiet he almost thought he'd imagined it. He frowned and hung up. ◇The phone immediately rang again. Once. Twice. Three times. Andrew's pulse quickened. He snatched up the receiver. "This isn't funny," he snapped. "Who is this?" The humming was louder now — clearer — and even though he couldn't make out the melody, something about it made his skin crawl. "Stop calling me!" he shouted, slamming the phone down. For a moment, silence filled the room. Then — one single ring. ◇The phone clicked itself to speaker mode. Andrew froze. The small digital display blinked: **UNKNOWN CALLER.** Before he could move, the screen glitched. The pixels flickered into a distorted image — *something* looking back at him, eyes wide and colorless, mouth stretched open mid-hum. A sharp burst of static shot through the speaker. Andrew stumbled backward, falling hard onto the couch as the phone slid from the table and hit the floor with a crack.

Elijah and Elias

The twins' house had been quiet all morning — too quiet. Elijah was brushing his teeth when the bathroom mirror fogged up on its own. He wiped it with a towel. Words appeared, written: **"WE SEE YOU"**

He stumbled back, calling for Elias. When his brother rushed in, the mirror had cleared — but the same words now stretched across the window. Elias turned, eyes wide. "It's on the TV too." Every reflective surface in the room shimmered faintly — mirrors, picture frames, even the glass of their watch faces. The messages changed again and again, cycling through phrases: **THE HOLLOW KNOWS. RETURN WHAT WAS TAKEN. WE SEE YOU.**   The last one stayed.
Elias cried, "We have to put this page back— Now!"

The Reunion

By Monday morning, every one of them had something to report — and every one of them was terrified. They met on the corner across from Cedar Hollow Café. The lights inside were off. A single note was taped to the door: **CLOSED FOR REPAIRS** Tamia stared at it. "Repairs? That's what they call witchcraft now?" Faith folded her arms. "They're not in here anymore." Elijah nodded, his voice low. "Then there's only one place left." "The library," Maliyah said. Zech frowned. "You mean Greystone Public Library?" "The one and only," Faith responded.

Mila squeezed her sister's hand. "Do we have to?" Maliyah smiled softly. "We started this together. We'll finish it together." The group exchanged conflicted looks, then started down the fog thickened street toward Greystone Public Library.

Greystone Public Library – That Night

The front doors creaked open easily — too easily. Inside, the air was dry and cold, filled with the smell of dust and burnt herbs. They moved in silence through the main hall, their footsteps echoing. Somewhere above them, faint humming drifted through the rafters — the same melody that had haunted them since the café. "Upstairs," Elijah said in a low voice. "That's where they are." As they climbed, the humming grew clearer — joined by whispers, laughter, the rustling of pages turning themselves. At the top of the stairs, light flickered from the old archive room. They peeked through the doorway.

The three witches were there — now dry, pristine, and terrible. One stood by a candlelit table, holding the blackened book open. One traced symbols in the air with her finger. The third watched the door, her smile knowing, eyes faintly glowing red.

Faith's voice shook. "They're planning something." Maliyah clenched her fists. "Then we'll stop them." Elijah reached into his pocket and felt the heat of the torn page. Somewhere deep in the library, a clock struck midnight. The witches turned in unison — and smiled.

CHAPTER X

The Light in the Hollow

The moment the clock struck midnight, every candle in the archive room flared. The air rippled like heat off asphalt. "Hide!" Faith shouted. The kids dove behind shelves as a dark column of smoke shot upward, slamming into the ceiling. Papers whirled through the air like frantic birds. The witches began to rise, humming that same awful tune.

Their eyes glowed the color of rust, their shadows stretching longer than their bodies. Maliyah grabbed Mila's hand. "It's too dark— How do we stop them if we cant see!?" Zech switched on his phone flashlight. "Can you see me?" Within seconds, the room blazed with phone screens, headlamps, even Tamia's key-chain torch.

The witches hissed, smoke curling from their skin. Elijah felt the torn page pulsing in his pocket like a heartbeat. "The page is reacting to the light!" "Use it!" Faith cried. He lifted the page. Symbols flared, spinning into the air like molten gold. The witches screamed—voices rising until glass shattered across the room.

"Keep the light on them!" Maliyah yelled. Branden yanked a reading-lamp cord free, sparks bursting. Journey hit the wall switch, flooding the room with raw fluorescent light. The witches staggered, gray and cracking, their robes tearing like ash. Andrew threw the fuse box lever. Every light in Greystone Public Library blazed pure white. The witches shrieked once more as their forms dissolved into drifting dust. Then silence.

Aftermath

For a long moment, none of them moved. The air felt new—warm, alive.
The shelves gleamed. Windows shone clean. The chandeliers sparkled like crystal raindrops. Mila whispered, "It's beautiful." Maliyah nodded. "We did it!" Tamia grinned. "Guess we're officially ghost hunters now." Zech laughed, still shaking. "Or extremely lucky middle-schoolers." Faith smiled. "Maybe both." They began to gather their scattered things when a soft sound drifted through the air—a Chime. Light and delicate, like a bell underwater.Mila tilted her head. "Did you hear that?" "Yeah," Elijah said softly. "Over there."

The Hidden Room

They followed the chime past the restored archive room into a shadowed corner where the shelves ended in a wall that didn't quite meet the ceiling. Dust coated old boxes stacked to the rafters. The chime came again—closer. Together they started moving boxes aside. Faith sneezed. Zech groaned. Mila giggled. And then, under a layer of cobwebs, something glimmered. A small, white key.

Journey picked it up carefully. "Looks ancient." "It fits here," Branden said, pointing to a narrow door half-hidden behind a book cart. The key turned with a soft *click*. Inside waited a tiny room lit by a single beam from the moonlight above. A round table stood in the center, scattered with dust-covered trophies, seashells, and yellowed newspaper clippings.

On the wall hung a framed photograph—children, maybe around their age, standing proudly beside the same table. Beneath it, carved into the wood: **THE INVESTIGATORS – 1953** For a long moment, no one breathed. Dust shimmered in the air like frozen time. Maliyah's voice broke the silence. "Wait... they had a team—just like us." Faith leaned closer, brushing her fingers over the faded carving. "This must've been their headquarters," she murmured. "It's like they left it behind for someone to find."

Mila found another old, tarnished photo frame from the desk. Inside, a group of smiling teens stood proudly beside a "Greystone Investigators" banner. "They were real," she whispered. "Look—there's a whole team." Zech squinted at the photo. "Crazy. They look our age." Elijah leaned in. "Hold up—count them. There's six." Faith frowned. "No... there's only five." Everyone looked again.

One spot in the photo was faint, the image blurred where a sixth figure should have been. Before anyone could speak,

the air shifted—soft, warm, and humming with quiet light. The lamps flickered once, and when they steadied, she was standing there. A girl, maybe sixteen, in a 1950s school uniform—hair tied with a ribbon, her presence glowing faintly like the morning sun through fog. Her smile was gentle, but her eyes carried decades of knowing. "Hello," she said, voice calm and melodic. "I'm Evelyn Wren. I was one of them." The group gasped—Mila stumbled back, clutching Faith's arm.

Branden yelped, "Okay—nope, nope, we're talking to a ghost! A *nice* ghost, I think—but still a ghost!" Evelyn smiled faintly. "You don't have to be afraid. I've waited a long time for someone to find this place again." Maliyah stepped forward, her fear fading beneath curiosity. "You were one of the Investigators?" Evelyn nodded. "Yes. We tried to protect Greystone... but some things we couldn't stop. You can." Her gaze swept across them, soft but firm. "You're the next chapter. The Hollow Heroes."

Tamia's voice shook. "Are you... here to help us?" Evelyn's smile brightened, her outline shimmering like candlelight. "Until the curse is broken, yes. You'll see me again—when you're ready." The lamps dimmed, a faint wind stirring the papers around them. When the light steadied again, she was gone.

Mila glanced at the photo on the desk—Evelyn's figure now completely missing. Zach blinked. "Okay, that's officially the coolest—and creepiest—thing that's ever happened to me." Branden exhaled, still wide-eyed. "Cool? Dude, I nearly passed out!" Maliyah smiled despite the shock. "Then I guess we're not alone in this." Outside, the fog lifted from the windows, revealing the moon above Greystone's spires. Inside, the glow of the lamps softened, warm and steady—a promise. Somewhere beyond the walls, a faint bell chimed once more. And this time, it didn't sound like an ending. It sounded like a beginning.

Epilogue

Morning sunlight spilled across the steps of Greystone Public Library. A Closed for the Season sign now hung on the gate while restoration crews packed up their tools. Down below, in their new hidden room, the children worked excitedly—pinning newspaper clippings, sketching maps, and taping handwritten signs that read **THE INVESTIGATORS: RE-OPENED**. Tamia adjusted her glasses. "We've got new reports already. Strange lights near the lighthouse. Whispers under the boardwalk." Maliyah smiled. "Greystone never stays quiet for long." Mila hugged her plush cat. "Good. I like being an Investigator." Zech laughed. "You'll change your mind when our next case starts crawling." They all burst out laughing, their voices filling the once-dark library with warmth. Above them, the chandelier chimed softly—a faint, friendly echo of the light that had saved them.

Across Town

The seagulls drifted inland on the sea breeze, passing over Blackwood Hollow Academy. The campus lay still—buildings silent, courtyard empty. The long weekend had left the school deserted. But inside... The faint echo of footsteps broke the silence. A single figure walked the corridor — tall, deliberate, dressed in black from collar to boot. The light from the windows didn't touch him; it bent away, leaving his face hidden in shifting shadow. His every step rippling through the halls like a slow applause.

The windows trembled, glass shuddering in their frames, as though the building itself could feel his presence. Dark, smoky shapes bled from the corners of the ceiling — hands, long-fingered and thin, not reaching to harm, but lowering, bowing as he moved. The figure paused at the center of the main hall. For a moment, he stood perfectly still, the dim light tracing the sharp outline of his shoulders, the faint rise of a smile. Then, a sound—low, deliberate laughter—rolled through the corridor. Not manic. Not loud. Just confident. Every light flickered once, then steadied.

And he kept walking, the sound of his boots fading deeper into the academy's heart.

To Be Continued....Book Two

A SALUTE

From our military family to yours—thank you.

To the service members—

Active Duty, Guard, Reserve, and Veterans—who raise a hand and keep raising it, day after day: your courage is more than moments; it's a steady, quiet promise. We honor your discipline, your sacrifice, and the way you carry the weight so others can breathe easy. To the spouses and partners who keep the home front humming—who learn new towns, new time zones, new schools; who handle midnights, repairs, and first days without your person; who pack and unpack and somehow make every house a home—you are strength in motion. To the children with brave hearts and heavy backpacks—professional new-kid greeters, quick-friend makers, memory keepers—you teach us resilience with every goodbye and hello. You are heroes, too. May this book feel like a small bit of light you can carry anywhere—a little light for late nights, long waits, and new beginnings. With gratitude and respect, from one military family to all the others: we see you, we honor you, and we're cheering you on.

To My Loving Husband, Roosevelt—
Your love is the steady rhythm beneath these pages. You encouraged every idea, listened to every new scene, and believed in my voice from the very start. You stood beside me—patient, proud, and present—and your confidence in my gift never wavered. This book carries our love in every chapter. Thank you for being my Husband, my best friend, my heart, my safe place, my everything.

To My Beautiful Daughters, Maliyah and Mila—
My girls, my heart, my reason. You are the pulse inside this story. You've crossed oceans and schools, learned new streets and new routines, always with a brave smile and understanding. Thank you for walking with me through each move, for letting boxes become castles, for turning new towns into adventures, for curling up beside me while I typed and asking, "What happens next?" Thank you for lending your names and your light to the girls on these pages, for the drawings, the ideas, the late-night giggles, the proud "That's us!" when a scene felt right. You gave my story a heartbeat. You remind me every day that home is not a place we unpack; it's the love we carry together." I love you girls so much.

To My Mother-In-Law, Barbara—
From the beginning of the love I share with your son, you met me with patience, kindness, and strength. When I lost my mother, you stood beside me with a mother's heart and a best friend's care. Thank you for loving me as your own.

—Love Always

To our *family and friends* who have been so supportive, read early pages, or simply asked, "How's the book going?"—you kept the wind in these sails. To the *teachers, librarians, and booksellers* who place stories into the right hands—you change lives, one reader at a time. And to you, *the reader*—thank you for stepping into Greystone and walking these halls with us. If **Book One** made you peek over your shoulder, or stay up one chapter longer, then it did its job. If it *felt like your kind of story,* please share it with a friend. I can't wait to welcome you back for **Book Two**—the doors to Blackwood Hollow are still accepting enrollment packets.

ABOUT THE AUTHOR

M.P. Glenn is a dreamer, storyteller, and believer in the quiet magic that lives in everyday moments. Inspired by her children's boundless imagination and curiosity, she writes stories that celebrate courage, friendship, and the wonder of discovering new worlds — both real and imagined.

Her debut series, Welcome to Greystone: The Chilling Tales of Blackwood Hollow Academy, invites readers on adventures filled with mystery, laughter, and heart. Through her writing, Glenn hopes to remind readers that even the simplest moments — a shared smile, a whispered secret, or a brave first step — can hold a little bit of magic.

When she isn't writing, she enjoys traveling, sketching new ideas, and spending time with her family, who continue to inspire the characters and stories she creates. To her, storytelling is more than words on a page — it's a way of capturing love, imagination, and the spark of wonder that connects us all.

www.ingramcontent.com/pod-product-compliance
Lightning Source LLC
Chambersburg PA
CBHW060337310726
48976CB00007B/2597